Purple and Other Hues

Also by Barbara Gurney and published by Ginninderra Press
Footprints of a Stranger
Life's Shadows

Barbara Gurney

Purple and Other Hues

Author's note

These stories are just a few of the hundreds written since joining Gosnells Writers Circle (2008) and Writefree Women's Writing Group (2009). Most have been inspired by themes suggested by these writing groups. Some have a hint of realism tucked into the pages, but all persons are of my imagination. If your personality peeks through the writing, I only hope you will be pleased.

Purple and Other Hues
ISBN 978 1 76041 516 7
Copyright © text Barbara Gurney 2018

First published 2018 by
Ginninderra Press
PO Box 3461 Port Adelaide 5015
www.ginninderrapress.com.au

Contents

Awards

The following stories have won awards:

'Purple' – First Prize, Yarram Community Learning
Centre Annual Literary Competition 2012

'Wide Brown Land' – First Prize, Minlaton
Show Literary Awards 2012

'Colour of Courage' – First Prize, Geelong Writers
Flash Fiction Writing Competition 2015

'By Darkened Shore' – Shortlisted, Raspberry &
Vine Short Story Competition 2012

Purple

As I sit in this busy café, I hold a gift in my hand. The silver box is bound by a luxurious white ribbon. It seems a shame to spoil the elegant effect with eager tugging. The card wishes me Happy Birthday and I thank my friend for her expression of love. I lift the lid and soft folds of patterned silk spill onto the table.

The surrounding noises become an instant mumble. They could be sounds of foreign places because I feel separated by the language of confusion. If someone reached out to touch me at this very moment, I'm sure their hand would go right through me. The nothingness makes me close my eyes – and the memories return.

Family photographs fill in the missing pieces from my remembered childhood. Each frozen moment tells a story, but sometimes the story shifts – depending on which part of the picture is important at the time. And so it is with Angela and me.

It seemed Angela had always been there. Just fifteen months younger than me, my sister was entwined in all my celebrations and most of my childhood adventures.

My earliest memory was of another bed being crammed into my bedroom. I pushed my few dresses to the right-hand end of the wardrobe and happily hung up my four-year-old sister's clothes.

Mum unearthed matching canary-yellow bed covers and we draped them around our bodies, parading ceremoniously in front of Dad before dragging them along the passageway, picking up minute bundles of fluff, until we rolled onto our beds still curled up inside the soft expectations of togetherness.

Dad bought us a bright pink mat scattered with odd red circles which we decided were badly blown-up balloons. The mat signalled the start of sharing, as it bridged the distance between our beds.

The first night, a sliver of light peeked into our room offering a glow of comfort, as Mum had left the door ajar.

Giggling started about twenty seconds after Mum whispered, 'Goodnight, darlings. God bless.'

Then Angela bounced on my bed and pulled at the covers. 'Let me in, let me in.' She didn't wait for approval and snuggled down against me, bumping her knees into my stomach.

I placed my arm around her chest and tickled her back – not enough to make her laugh, but soft noises of delight blew into my ear in puffs as delicate as thistles' seed-heads drifting in a breeze. We fell asleep tightly woven, but woke with our arms and legs spread out, imitating the letter X. I pushed Angela gently and told her to go back to her bed.

She refused and pulled the pillow from under my head and leaned against it. With her arms folded, she pouted, 'I like yours best.'

The second night, I followed her into the bathroom, announcing I was ready for sleep even though it was an hour before my official bedtime. We cleaned our teeth without soliciting and Dad was surprised to have two pyjama-clad daughters, smelling of talc, wriggling on his knee, eager to say goodnight.

'What's this?' he asked as Angela rubbed her fingers across the stubble on his chin. 'Two sleepy angels.'

I poked him in the middle of his stomach and said, 'You've only one angel, Daddy. I'm Laura.'

Giving our mother a quick sideways glance, he said, 'Only one? No, I have two beautiful angels – and both had better be on their way before I decide they've had their last hug ever.'

Our arms smothered him and we covered his ever-increasing forehead in kisses before simultaneously sliding from his lap, racing down the passage and colliding in one bed.

'Now, girls, what's wrong with the other one?' Mum asked knowingly.

'But, Mum…' Angela whined as she held onto my sleeve.

'Okay, as long as I don't hear a sound out of you. Otherwise it's into the other bed for one of you.'

When the novelty of retiring early wore off, I would promise to join Angela later. Sometimes I did, often I didn't. However, she was always beside me by the morning. She could never tell me when she had changed beds – she'd just shake her head and announce that the sleeping fairy had moved her.

Years went by and we did eventually sleep separately. However, if she was scared of a storm which made the hibiscus scratch against the window as if a witch was trying to get in and take us away on her broomstick, Angela would dart under my bedcovers and cuddle in against my back.

Whenever there were snippets of gossip to be shared, we would pull the doona over our heads and whisper away until sleep took over.

Angela had the habit of bringing her favourite doll into my bed on a Saturday morning.

'Sharing the caring,' Mum said when she found me reading a book to my seven-year-old sister and a blank-faced doll with crooked green lipstick.

We celebrated my eleventh birthday with a day at the beach. By early afternoon, Angela complained about feeling hot and cold at the same time. The chocolate cake with unlit candles stayed in the pantry when she went to bed at half-past four. I sulked about missing out on the cake, but Mum was too busy worrying about Angela, and Dad told me the cake would still be there tomorrow, when we could all share it.

Throughout the night I could hear Angela moaning and my parents whispering as they sat with her. I found it hard to sleep and eventually sat on the edge of my bed, biting the side of my mouth and picking my thumbnail until it bled. Dad told me to go and sleep in their room, but that made me fear the worst. If they weren't prepared to leave her, there had to be something wrong.

I fell asleep leaning on Dad and he tucked me into their bed, where I slept until I woke to a siren shrieking into our driveway.

Trying to make sense of the pandemonium, I watched Mum crying and Dad doing his best not to. The creases in his forehead kept changing as his eyebrows went up and down. One moment he stood with his arm around Mum, the next he was shoving his hands into his pockets and taking small steps towards the front door.

'Dad, what's happening?'

I ran to him and he clutched me, hugging me to his side. Mum gripped my arm and her fingers dug in and made me squeal. I found it strange that my kind-hearted mother didn't apologise but squeezed even tighter.

Two men with a stretcher came out from my bedroom. Our pink mat was caught in the wheel and Dad snatched at it, pulled it away and threw it behind me. It lay crumpled, and I thought the balloons might burst if the mat weren't straightened. Then I realised my sister was on the trolley. Opaque tubes made her seem distorted and colourless.

'Angie!' I screamed.

Dad hung his head and gave up trying not to cry.

The moment became a jigsaw strewn across a table. Nothing seemed to fit. There was an understanding of the importance of each singular piece, but the whole picture had been destroyed.

Dad held my hand and told me I would have to be his brave angel. His voice crackled like an old radio as he explained Mum would be going with Angela to the hospital and he would follow later, as soon as Aunt Janey arrived.

'Let me come too,' I cried.

'I'm sorry, darling, but you can't. The doctors and nurses will look after her. We'll take you to see her as soon as she's better.'

I stared at my father as if he were a stranger. 'No, Dad, Angie needs me if she's in pain. I can stroke her head and tickle her feet. I can make her feel better.'

He held me so tightly I thought I would pop out of his arms like a slippery piece of soap, but his cheek fell against the top of my head and I heard noises I couldn't recognise.

At that moment, the ambulance officer called to my father. I spilled from his grip and both of us ran to the back of the vehicle. While Dad answered rapid questions and shot off questions of his own, I stood on tiptoe and looked at Angela. Her pyjama top was scrunched under the tubes and I could see splotches of purple on her skin.

'Dad, why is Angela purple? What did she spill?'

They closed the doors and the ambulance rushed away from Dad and me.

Later, Mum sobbed as she explained our beautiful angel had turned purple almost before their eyes. The pathways of sneaking indigo and violet, which make rainbows so pretty, crawled around her and, despite frantic treatment, she succumbed within hours.

Dad told me Angela would always be our special angel. I looked at my feet and reminded him he said he had two angels. He gripped me by both arms, said nothing, but pulled me into his chest and kept hold until I wriggled for release.

Every time I closed my eyes, I saw purple veins spreading over my eyelids. Neon lights flashing from shop windows all seem to be that vile colour. Baskets standing outside a grocery store glorified purple flowers. I hated them instantly.

The largest pair of scissors I could find helped me destroy my newest dress – I could no longer stand the purple patterns zigzagging across the fabric like the lightning which had caused Angela to leap into my bed. Mum found me surrounded by jagged pieces of cloth, determined to cut them even smaller. I snipped off a piece of my fringe because I wanted to see the destruction more clearly.

'Laura, dear, what a thing to do.' Mum took away the scissors and held me at arm's length for just a second, trying to see if a piece of my heart could be saved from the torment. Then she wrapped her arms around me and we cried together.

'I *hate* purple.'

'Yes, darling. We all do.'

The following week, a rotund teddy arrived home with Dad. It had one black eye; the other one was brown and sewn slightly higher than its partner.

'Just for you, Laura. It can keep you company. Might even be a comfy pillow.'

'He's…different. Why does he have odd eyes?'

Dad turned the teddy around and held it five centimetres from his face. 'Doesn't matter. He's jolly good-looking, I reckon.' He chuckled as he passed it back to me. 'Does he get a name?'

Ignoring Dad's attempt at humour, I tucked the toy under my arm. 'He's rather big. I could call him Big Ted, I suppose.'

I wasn't old enough then to understand it was a gift of their hope. Hope that both their daughters wouldn't be ruined by one illness.

Dad intended to remove Angela's bed, but I wouldn't let him because I couldn't be sure which was hers and which was mine. Some nights, I lay in the dark asking Angie if I had chosen the bed she didn't want – just like when she was alive. Big Ted usually sat on the empty one.

One night, I thought Big Ted might be nice to cuddle, but he didn't have long soft curls to snake around my fingers. There were no toes to pinch my legs and make me try to pinch back. I tickled his padded tummy, I even forced a giggle, but there was no response. I slung him across the room and heard him thump against the wall. For a moment, I was glad he was upside down, with his lopsided eyes jammed against the plaster, but I thought of Angie and her favourite doll, and climbed out into the cold to sit Big Ted alongside Sally-Ann and hoped he liked ladies with green lipstick.

Years wandered through sad days, occasionally springing surprises of joyous moments and turning the weeks into bearable measures of time. Happiness began to wrap around the gloom, making it tolerable. Memories became like collections of trinkets, gathering dust, but unable to be discarded.

And so I come back to this place, this day, this time where emotions are exposed. I accidentally knock my cup and the dark dregs slosh against the stark white sides until the moment passes and it remains safe within its confines. I cause the face of my friend to disappear into a shroud of indifference and the noises of the people around us turn into superfluous commotion. I sag in my seat and stare at the face of my friend again – a face which now seems too close; too needy.

The wide purple threads reach across the scarf spoiling the creaminess of the background. It suddenly drips over the edge of the table and spills onto my knee. I stop it from falling onto the floor where I could strike it with my shoe – leave grime and dirt across its width. A scratchy sound makes me pull my fingernail away quickly – I could tear at its pattern, ruin it in an instant, but nothing will banish the malicious colour.

The silk is cold, a pleasant cold, like an autumn morning after a hot summer. My fingers feel the luxury of the material as it works its way round my thumb and cascades over my palm. I wind the scarf into a purple-streaked rosette and place it back in the box.

I close my eyes again and force the memories away.

Rust

Leaves brush gently against my roof. Loose flakes of rust cling momentarily to the surface then are whisked away.

I no longer chug with pleasure or move on demand.

The absence of a bonnet exposes my soul.

I remember the joy of hard work. My usefulness was in strength. I took pride in my reliability.

Now daises grow around my aged, deflated tyres – perished beyond roadworthiness.

One windscreen wiper falls, slipping into the depths of the weeds. Groans of old age echo across the quiet paddocks.

I see a figure striding towards me.

She stops, grins, as she looks me over.

She's young and eager, with a camera slung over her shoulder.

She runs her hand over my dented panel before stepping back.

'Smile,' she jokes as she points the lens at me.

Pink Pearl

Wriggling the key into the lock, Pink glanced at the sign above the shop window: Pink's Millinery Boutique. Today, the feeling of pride mingled with dread. She pushed open the door, hurried past the display of gloves and bracelets, dropped her handbag below the counter and carefully placed the muslin bag, which held two large hats, on the workbench.

They were the last of an order of eight. Pink had spent long evenings stitching a yard of satin onto the brim of each one. A dozen tiny white roses now sat in the puckered cloth. She eased the hats out of the bag. The huge brim would be ideal in the sun, but these were for bridesmaids.

'The photographs will be interesting,' the milliner told a mannequin. 'No one will see their faces.'

Ladies were wearing smaller hats these days – ones that hugged the head, showing off their well-groomed hair. This bride could obviously afford to spend big, so why she wanted to have such terribly old-fashioned monstrosities baffled Pink.

During the war, materials had been scarce, and designers quickly altered their styles. Pink's exclusive designs were popular with the wealthy ladies of Perth, who wandered down London Court during their weekly shopping trip. When times became even tougher, restyling old hats had helped keep her ledger balanced. But now, with the well-established trend to go hatless, Pink wondered how long she could stay in business.

Two weeks ago, a new customer had strolled into the shop. Adeline Lavers lowered her nose long enough to introduce herself. 'I must have this fabric,' she said several times, as she fingered another expensive sample draped across the table.

With Miss Lavers dithering over selection, Pink was forced to abandon a regular customer.

Miss Lavers tried on practically every hat in the shop, and ridiculed the catalogue of designs. 'None is quite right. Don't you have any very large hats, Miss…'

'Miss Pink.'

'Really? That's a colour, not a name, surely.'

Pink answered with a sigh, 'It's certainly a colour, but it's also my name.'

'Well, maybe it's an omen. Do you have the voile in pink?'

Her father had named her Nora after his deceased sister. Mother insisted on adding Pearl. 'That way,' she said, 'I'll always have a pearl, no matter how poor we are.'

Father chuckled as he ran his finger under the chubby chin of his new daughter then brushed a feather of a kiss on her cheek. Mr Pinkington stood back, tucked his arm around his wife's waist and said he hoped their child would like pink pearls. From that moment, no one had called her anything but Pink.

Miss Lavers left without paying a deposit, but, being so keen to secure the large sale, Pink agreed to purchase the necessary stock and wait for the money.

Miss Lavers rang at closing time on Friday. Without a greeting, she said, 'I want to know if you've finished my order.'

Pink drew in a quick breath. 'No. I haven't received your deposit.'

'I'll pay it all together. Much easier. I don't want to have to go to the bank twice. Anyway, they're closed until Monday.'

'But…I've had to lay out money to get started.'

'Well,' Miss Lavers snorted, 'you'll just have to finish quickly. I'll be in next week. I expect them to be finished.' She didn't wait for a reply.

Several moments passed before Pink placed the phone back on its cradle. This order would enable her to pay the rent for another month. Her hats were admired, but sales continued to decline and the landlord demanded timely payment.

'If you can't pay, you can't have the shop. It's that easy,' Joe had said as he waved the rent book in front of his tenant's face. 'You have until the end of this month or it's curtains.'

'But, Joe, I've been here for years. Surely you know I'll pay.'

'I don't knows that, Miss Pink. Times are changin'. Me missus has one hat for church. She ain't buying a new one any time soon. Guess others won't be either.'

'Look, Joe. I'll have the money when this order is completed.'

'Well, it'd better come good. Real soon like. I've got another offer for this place.'

Pink's eyes widened. 'Never! Who?'

'It's those from next door. They want to expand, like. Reckon they're on to a good thing. Want more space.'

She couldn't believe it. Premier Business Service had only been in the shop six months. But after Joe's comment she recalled how an uppity young chap had walked through her shop last week. He'd announced he was from next door, ran his hand over the counter and enquired about the size of the back room.

'None of your business,' she'd answered.

'Maybe not, but then again, maybe it will be.' He'd pushed his hands into his pockets and strolled out the door.

Joe tapped the rent book on Pink's arm. 'Well, you get that money to me by the thirtieth and we'll be all sweet.'

She spent most of the afternoon calculating her expenditure for the Lavers sale. She'd purchased a twenty-yard roll of satin, base material for nine hats (one to work as a sample), countless roses, five rolls of ribbon, cards of lace, three yards of tulle and matching silk thread. As the warehouse wouldn't allow cut yardage, expenses were high and the remaining materials wouldn't be used immediately.

The days dragged on. Most sales were for small items: costume jewellery, a scarf, or the occasional pair of gloves.

Each time the door opened, Pink hoped it would be Miss Lavers. The finished hats lined the shelf behind the counter and she often tweaked the tulle as she waited. Two young ladies wanted to try on 'one of those silly hats – just for a laugh'. She enjoyed watching them parade between the display cabinets. At least someone was benefiting from the embarrassing creations that looked like wedding cakes. After they left, she moved Miss Lavers' hats to the back room and covered them with a sheet.

The unpleasant manager from Premiers stopped at her door every morning and afternoon, gazed in past the displays, nodded several times, and then moved away. Pink hated the smirk that crossed his freckled face as he rattled keys in his pocket. The routine was intolerable.

Deciding to confront him, she clipped her door and approached Premier's shop. The business ran a secretarial service and employment agency, along with selling the latest style of typewriter. Dozens of women were in and out of the place every day.

Pink peeked in through the small window. Leaning on the counter, Premier's manager watched his customers closely. She hesitated. Could she challenge this arrogant chap when he was surrounded by people? As one woman left, the person behind the counter came into view.

'What's she doing in there?' Pink's shaking fingers gripped the window frame. The self-important air of Adeline Lavers was on full display as she grabbed cash and ticked off names with an exaggerated flourish. The tip of Pink's nose touched the window, her quick breath fogged up the glass. 'Can't be her.' She turned and leaned against the wall.

'Excuse me, are you okay?' A young woman touched Pink's shoulder. 'Can I help you?'

'Is that…I mean…well, do you work here?'

'Yes, I started last week.'

The milliner watched the activity inside for a moment, then said, 'That woman…the one taking the money, who's she?'

'You mean Mrs Backshall. She's the manager's wife. Only comes in once a month to check on things.'

'Mrs? Mrs Backshall! Not Miss Lavers?'

The young woman shook her head. 'Sorry, I don't know a Lavers. Look, I've got to go in.'

Confused and vulnerable, Pink shuffled away. There was no wedding. It had all been a ruse to make sure expenses couldn't be recovered. They wanted to expand. They'd be taking over her shop.

She was still crying when her friend Ruth called in.

'How am I going to survive?' Pink asked. 'I need to pay Joe in ten days.'

'You'll think of something.'

'But hats aren't selling.'

'Then make something else. Something ladies can't do without.'

Ruth helped unpick the unwanted hats. They ironed the shiny material, ribbon and lace. They stayed late into the night, cutting, stitching and decorating the stored rolls of satin. Ten days later, the millinery shop became Pink's Boutique, with the revamped window displaying luxurious undergarments – pretty slips, and camisoles with discreetly folded panties, in elegant boxes.

Pink employed two assistants and when the rooms next door became available, Joe gave her a special rate. He wanted to recover lost rent as quickly as possible. It seemed Miss Lavers…Mrs Backshall…couldn't be trusted with the accounts.

Pink still designs fashionable millinery for wealthy clients. In fact, the mayor's daughter ordered one for her travelling outfit after her elaborate wedding. She'd remembered trying on a particularly large hat 'just for fun'. The bride-to-be and her friend had giggled all the way to the bus stop, promising they'd go back one day and have a hat Made by Pink.

Framed

It was no McCubbin, but it was meticulously painted. The artist had selected the colours carefully. The green leaves of the tall gum tree, the greying weatherboard timbers of a farmhouse, and the grasses – dry, ready to burn – all reflected an Australian landscape perfectly. I liked it instantly.

'How much for the painting?' I asked, as I peered at the signature.

'Make me an offer,' the woman replied.

'It's rather good.'

'It's my father-in-law's. We have to get rid of some of them. The old codger wants to keep them all. Not possible.'

I picked up the painting. 'Would you take fifteen dollars?'

'Nah. Wanted twenty. Frames cost money, you know.'

The hideous frame would be the first to go. 'Okay, twenty it is.'

With the painting, a few books and a large flowerpot on the back seat of my car, I left the garage sale and headed for the garden centre. The thought of my newly decorated family room made me smile. It was coming along a treat. The painting would look great on the panelling and match the soft outback tones of the curtains. Some plants near the back door and it would be finished.

The following afternoon, the phone rang. I removed my gardening gloves and hurried inside.

A man's voice interrupted my greeting. 'Look here. You took me dad's picture. I need it back.'

'Excuse me! Who is this?'

'Me name's Mike. Me wife said you're the one. The woman who took the picture of the house.' He grunted between sentences.

I frowned. 'I paid your wife for the painting. I'm not about to return it.'

'Yeah, well, I'd like it back.'

'She said you wanted to get rid of them.'

'Yeah, but not that one. The old man is furious. Said it's valuable. Got to get it back.'

I peered through the French doors and across the family room. The painting looked at home on my wall, but the frame definitely needed to be replaced. 'I've already hung it and I'll certainly not return it. Anyway, how did you get my number?'

'Our neighbour knows you. Saw you leaving.' He grunted again. 'I'll give you your money back.'

'I'm not interested in getting my money back. It was a fair transaction.'

I heard him protesting as I hung up.

The next Saturday, I came home to signs of intrusion. The side gate was open, and someone had trampled the flowers in the garden bed under my kitchen window. I called the police. They weren't interested unless something had been stolen.

Sunday night, a dog's demanding bark woke me. A car pulled away. I went back to sleep.

Monday. When I opened my front door, Mike's wife adjusted her handbag and looked down at her sneakers.

'Yes,' I said.

She stopped chewing her lip, forced a smile, then asked, 'I wonder if you might let us have that painting back?'

I kept the security door clipped, sighed loudly. 'The answer is still no. No, no, no. Can't either of you get that through your head?'

'You don't understand. The old chap is going off his head. He hasn't settled in the nursing home at all. Keeps hassling the staff. Won't eat.'

'That's unfortunate, but it has nothing to do with me. Go away.'

She let her bag drop to the ground as she pulled her cardigan across her chest. 'We have to have it. You see, Mike's dad insists it's more valuable than all the others. Please, we'll let you have another one, two maybe.'

The desperation in her eyes made me pause, my mind going back over the weekend. 'Your husband hasn't been taking things into his own hands, has he?'

'I don't know what you mean.'

'A matter of gaining the painting by foul means perhaps?'

Her desperation turned to fear. She snatched up her bag and tucked it under her arm. 'You'll hear from Mike. He wants the painting back.' She looked me up and down, turned around and stalked off down the path.

When I heard a noise in my backyard at two a.m., I rang the police again. 'Come quickly,' I whispered. 'Someone is trying to break in.'

They got them. Mike dressed in black with a glass-cutter in his hand, his wife shining a torch light through the window.

She glared at me as the police placed the handcuffs around her wrists.

'It's a wonderful painting.' I smirked. 'Quite valuable. Just as you said.'

Yesterday, when I'd removed the frame, I discovered dozens of hundred-dollar notes padding the painting. I couldn't decide between a Pacific cruise or one of those fancy river trips through Europe. Maybe even both.

I wondered what they told the old man.

Flames

Karla watched the flames dance around the twigs and over the large logs. The translucent smoke curled up the chimney. She shivered despite the radiant heat. How many times had she sat in front of this fire – alone?

Father was out in the falling snow, going somewhere unknown, doing whatever it was he did – a secret too covert to share with her.

'Better my young one doesn't know,' Vilic said many times.

When the door opened, a blast of freezing air shot across the room making the fire hesitate. Alerted by the complaining hinges, Karla jumped up from the cushion on the floor. She watched her father enter quickly then peer out through the last gap of the closing door.

'Father!'

'Hush a minute, child.'

He continued to watch. They both listened. When the footsteps disappeared beyond hearing, Vilic stood with his hand pressed hard against the closed door, waiting for his heartbeat to steady.

'Sorry, Karla,' he said as he removed his gloves, coat and scarf. 'I'm glad to be home.'

After exchanging his damp boots for slippers, he came towards her with his arms outstretched. She picked up a cushion and pulled it close to her chest. They stared at each other for a moment. Karla pouted.

Vilic's eyebrows lowered. 'What?' he shrugged.

She shoved the cushion at him. Her voice was quiet, but she spat out, 'You think I'm still a child. I'm fifteen.' She demanded, 'I want to know where you go.'

Vilic took the cushion placed it on the settee and sighed. 'Karla dear.'

She brushed his hand from her shoulder and turned away.

'Please, Karla, come, sit with me. I'll try to explain.'

He didn't need to explain their history. She remembered their home opposite Letna Park: the long velvet curtains, perfect for a game of hide-and-seek, Mother's kisses when she discovered her child, and the soft floor rug where she could play with her many toys. Karla also remembered her father's sadness when her mother died – his struggle when circumstances changed quickly and how he ensured she could continue her schooling, despite the authorities threatening to cancel her papers if he didn't cooperate. Vilic didn't want his daughter to end up working in the laundry of Russian diplomats.

'I don't need your futile explanations. I've heard them all before,' she said.

The long hours he spent away from her in the evenings were necessary, he said. It would make a difference, he said.

No, Karla didn't want justification for the odd telephone calls, the hurried departures and the furtive visitors. She just wanted her father to be home, to be sitting in front of the red and gold flames, reading, talking, perhaps even singing Mother's favourite songs. The authoritarian regime, the cramped accommodation and repetitive meals could be tolerated a little better when they were together.

She stood by the dresser, which squeezed between the settee and the table. There were only three chairs. The others hadn't been delivered with the rest of the furniture when they were forced to move. The tiny flats in a building with sixty-three families bred dissension and misery. Smiles were few as displaced persons passed each other on the noisy concrete stairs, each family unable to understand why a foreigner deserved their home in central Prague more than they did.

'Come, dear. Sit with me. Please, Karla.'

She bit her lip to stop it from trembling. Scrunched up in the corner of the settee, she looked sideways at her father.

'It won't be long. You'll see. Things will be different,' Vilic said.

Karla grabbed her father's arm. 'No, it won't!' she snapped. 'Nothing will change. They'll always be here. Always ruining our lives.'

He prised her fingers free and held them gently. 'I know, I know, my pet. It's difficult. We have to be patient.'

She wriggled up closer to him, laying her head against his shoulder, and said slowly, 'I was arrested today.'

'What?' He stood up and looked around the room as if someone might be lurking in the small space. He rearranged the curtains, making sure not a spot of light could escape. 'Arrested? Why? Tell me.' He sat down again and placed one hand on her knee.

Her tears started. She pushed his hand away. 'I was just coming home from school. There was a protest. Many university students. So much noise. Yelling and screaming. I couldn't get through the crowd.'

She wiped her eyes and sniffed noisily. He offered her his handkerchief.

'I was at the corner. Almost free of the rally. The police grabbed me.' She shivered. 'I didn't know what to do. I didn't know where you were. I was shoved along. Handcuffed.'

Vilic closed his eyes. He leaned forward, his head in his hands.

She continued to sniff, wiping her eyes and nose on the damp handkerchief. 'I tried to tell them that I was just going home. Not part of the protest. Not involved. They scrutinised my papers. They refused to believe me. I was forced to sit in a cold room for several hours.' Karla ran her fingernail up and down her arm. Red marks appeared.

'A young policeman gave me some water and whispered your name, told me he'd do what he could. In a loud voice, he told me to wait. I waited. Other people were brought in. No one spoke to me. I was frightened. Finally I was released. The kind policeman smiled behind his hand and told me to hurry home.'

Vilic fought tears, clenched his hands.

Karla's anger returned. 'Why couldn't I find you?'

He pulled at a resilient piece of fluff on his jumper. 'There was also a protest outside in the square.' He coughed, clearing emotion from his throat.

Karla asked, 'And?'

'I was there with Lucas. We stayed.' Vilic pushed his hands through his greying hair. 'Two young men were yelling for people to stop being complacent. "Stand up to the government," they yelled. They had cigarette lighters and gasoline. One dared the crowd to set them alight. "Palach, Palach," the crowd started chanting. People pushed forward. I could feel hands on my back.' Vilic stood up.

Karla ignored her tears.

He paced. 'The mood was volatile. We managed to get away. We ran past Palach's monument. We remembered his fight in 1969. How could we not?' Vilic licked at his tears. 'Palach, so brave.' He slapped his cheek trying to gain control. 'To allow flames to take one's life. For liberty of others. I can't imagine.' He shuddered as he sat down.

She took his hand.

'Lucas and I became separated,' he whispered.

He sat quietly. Karla gripped his hand tighter.

'Then, I came home.'

Fifteen days later, 250,000 Czech people demonstrated in Wenceslas Square, wearing gas masks, to express their feelings concerning the new government dominated by communists. The Velvet Revolution broke out in 1989 and in 1990 the first democratic elections for almost sixty years were held.

Karla poked at the fire.

Vilic poured the beer making sure it frothed to the top.

They celebrated quietly. He no longer had to go to his friend Lucas's basement each evening. Although there were still disparities, still people in need, they could plan without stealth.

Vilic could sit and watch the flames with Karla.

They might even sing.

White Ribbon

The first time the phone rang, she scampered across the room and said eagerly, 'Hello, this is Tania.'

Despite further prompting, the caller remained silent.

Just as she had settled back on the couch with a fresh coffee, and recommenced reading, it rang again.

She answered warily, 'Hello.'

A slight cough as the person cleared their throat; then…nothing.

Recognising the gravelly sound, Tania trembled, took a deep breath and said, 'I know it's you. I know you're there.' Tania heard rustling, some movement. Her voice shrieked with dread, 'Stop calling me?'

A nasty snigger preceded the click of rejection.

She stood with her hands on the kitchen bench, her head almost touching the flecked laminate. Her back ached, but she felt unable to move. The phone rang again. Tania counted the ring tones. 'One, two, three, four…'

She straightened her suffering back and reached for the offending phone which had ceased its torment. It rang again under her hand. 'Stop it!' she yelled into the mouthpiece. Then she yanked it from the wall. She stared at the detached instrument for a moment. Her hand shook. She gulped back tears. 'Leave me alone,' she cried as she threw the handpiece across the room.

Tania could feel the rough houndstooth pattern of the cushion biting into her leg. The scratching of the bougainvillea on the window sounded as if it scraped against her ear drum. Her breath was even but shallow, and her heart beat as loud as the bass drum of a military band. She rubbed one hand across the other forearm, feeling the bumps and raised hair. She read a half page without registering a single word. Her throat screamed for a drink, but she found it hard to swallow the tepid coffee.

Tania picked at her thumbnail; nibbled the torn nail. Her eyes darted from the kitchen window to the sliding doors leading to the back patio. It felt like her stomach had become dislodged in her throat. Bile snuck into her mouth. The cold coffee mixed with the bile and created an undrinkable liquid. She spat it back into the mug, shook her head, wiped her hand across her lips, tucked her legs up and hugged the cushion.

A car screeched to a halt in the street.

Tania became a statue.

The car pulled into her driveway.

She held her trembling lips between her teeth. Closed her eyes. No, no, don't let it be him, her mind screamed.

Footsteps crunched on the driveway. Reached the path. Became bullet-like.

Tania shuddered and opened her eyes, willing the locks on the front door to hold.

The doorbell jangled repeatedly. Her stomach somersaulted. She stared down the passage, singling out the door jamb and its hinges. She was sure her eyes would pop out of their sockets. The door shook as a fist hammered and thumped.

'What can I do?' she whispered, as the door wobbled in resistance.

Tania forced herself to breathe evenly as the swearing got softer. Finally, the hammering ceased. The car squealed away.

Silence touched the house again.

She buried her head in the cushion and let relief build.

Wide Brown Land

'I'm going,' Max said. 'I'll be out the back paddock, got to check the fence. See ya.'

'Bye, love, see you for lunch.' Julie waved as the quad bike started. 'Stay safe,' she yelled.

Buddy's tail wagged ceaselessly, flapping across the fumes from the exhaust, making spurts of smoke signals. Max rode alongside the boundary fence for ten minutes, turned left by the empty water tank and became a spot in Julie's vision. She stood with her arms folded across her chest, imagining Buddy poking his nose under Max's arm and Max telling the dog to 'Stop that' while what he really wanted to say was 'Thanks, mate.'

In the last few months, they had struggled with their emotions as the dry wind whipped up dust into circles of misery and blew with wicked intent across the empty paddocks. Their marriage remained strong, but it required a constant effort to buoy each other through the ever-burdening drought. They pushed individual dread behind a smile, scared lest once they spoke of the fear behind their false joy they would be sent into a bottomless pit of unrecoverable wretchedness.

Many evenings they sat reading as the hours ticked away until bedtime beckoned. If the wind momentarily ceased, they would pause from absorbing words and, with a glance at each other, hope that perhaps this time it was the calm before the long-awaited storm. Too many books had been read as they waited for rain – waiting to be saved from disaster. Their bookcase was full of other people's dreams bound into words for people like Max and Julie to read while they waited to fulfil their own dreams.

Julie knew it was useless to polish away the dust on the surfaces, but, just as Max was compelled to examine sturdy fences, she needed to be busy.

Picking up her husband's choice of reading from last night, it caught against the arm of the chair and fell to the floor.

'Damn!' She retrieved the open poetry book from the floor. '*My Country!* That's surely appropriate. By Dorothea Mackellar. I remember learning that at school.' Perched on the arm of the couch, Julie started reading. When she came to the second verse, the words became familiar. 'I love a sunburnt country.'

Her particular piece of countryside had been green when Julie arrived as a new bride. The property spread as far as the eye could see – from Bill Turner's fences in the north to the other side of Murchison Road. The old farmhouse, now theirs, stood tucked away at the far end of Max's family farm. She had been so proud. A farmer's wife! Yes, she wanted to live all her days in the country.

Julie read aloud, 'I love a sunburnt country, a land of sweeping plains.'

She rose from the chair and walked to the window. Pulling aside the curtains, she gazed into the distance. Somewhere on those 'sweeping plains' the love of her life would be driving the beat-up quad bike around the fence line looking for breaks. In the past few weeks, he had been relentlessly drawn to this mundane and unnecessary routine. The hand-feeding of their stock didn't take up all his time, and Max had to do something or he would go mad. Circling his precious ground brought mixed emotions: glad to be active, sad to see the topsoil slowly disappearing in the hungry wind.

Julie let the curtains drop as she leaned against the door frame. She tucked one hand under her hair and twirled it around her damp fingers. Then, releasing the long brown strands, she shook her head, making her hair flick backwards and forwards across closed eyes. She dug her fingernails into the soft cover of the small book and sighed. It had to rain soon; she couldn't stand this heat much longer.

Outside, a magpie squawked with delight as it found something to eat under her withering passionfruit vine and she watched him fly off into the cloudless blue sky of summer.

'Of ragged mountain ranges,' she read.

There were hardly any mountains in this part of the sun-drenched country. A few rocky outcrops ran along their boundary and her eyes scanned the distance for the closest ones which broke up the monotony of the flat paddocks. A mirage of water ran in a shimmering line below the scattered rocks, just beneath the horizon.

When the children were small, they would often take a picnic out to those rocks. Spring rain would make little puddles ideal for Michael and Oliver to splash in. Wild flowers would cover the edges of the outcrop, making a bountiful scene which the young boys failed to appreciate. But they loved to toss rocks as far as they could. It was Julie and Max's task to find the thrown rock and yell encouraging sounds back to the boys. They consumed cold roast lamb sandwiches, fruit from the backyard garden and warming cordial in a hurry so another game could be invented.

Only the lizards would be enjoying the hot rocks today; sunning themselves until evening fell, turning the ground cold and unforgiving. Julie could feel the heat rising in the room and she flapped the book in an attempt to move some air. Recommencing the reading brought a lump to her throat, and the words came out in broken pieces of longing.

'Of ragged mountain ranges, of droughts and flooding rains.'

If only, thought Julie. A flood, I could handle right now. They were fed up with this drought. Nerves were frayed within a breath of snapping. They checked long-range forecasts daily and the computer became used to being sworn at in a fury of frustration.

Farmers prayed for rain. Farmers' wives prayed for the farmers.

If rain came, Max wouldn't have to aimlessly scour the fences pretending to be attentive when he was really dreaming of green pastures and fat sheep. Julie would then be happier to go to town and spend time with other wives from the district. As it was, they were all too scared to be honest with each other. You could see it in their faces. They guarded their words. Hesitant to talk of farming matters – skirting stock and feed issues, while adding flippant comments not believed by the listeners.

With the book clenched in one hand, Julie wandered into the kitchen and flicked the switch for another cup of tea. As the power surged into the water the next line presented itself.

'I love her far horizons.'

She placed the book next to the kettle and pushed the back door open. The stiff wind flung pieces of leaf litter at her, causing her to squint. She could just see the sheep that were causing the dry dirt to billow into the air as they searched the remains of the morning's feed.

Max was out there somewhere. He had been away for over an hour. Yes, he would be in the east paddock by now. Beyond the house yard, beyond the barren paddocks and past the fence that Max would have checked, was that magical line called the horizon.

She recited the next line off by heart, 'I love her jewel-sea.'

Their family had holidayed at Byron Bay before it became the trendy place of today. The cool waters were always a shock as one tiptoed into the unfamiliar blue liquid. The boys loved the waves, which threatened to up-end them when their backs were turned. They let sandcastles wash away in the afternoon tide and contentedly strolled to the corner shop for ice cream.

'Jewel seas, yes, that's a very apt description,' Julie declared as she dipped the teabag in and out of the steaming cup of water. She acknowledged that the few times they had taken a holiday from the farm, she'd been excited by it all, but always ready to come home – pleased to be in her own kitchen, her own bed, but most of all to be surrounded by the gum trees and sheep paddocks.

She returned to the compelling lines of the poem.

'Her beauty and her terror.'

The simple line of the poem scattered multiple images as she considered the diversity of Australia. With seaside frivolity left behind, one can be in the midst of farming territory in a few short hours. Each person sees beauty in different scenes, but every mile of this huge country is worth exploring. From the glorious sunset-filled beaches of the western boundary, across the central deserts, to tree-lined Blue Mountains of the east, one can experience a unique environment. The beauty of it all surely outweighs the threat of dangers like bushfires, cyclones and floods. Monstrous crocodiles, dangerous spiders and the notorious snakes all had a part to play in the make-up of this unique land.

Julie stood outside the kitchen door, now oblivious to the oppressive heat. She turned the little book over and reread each line of the familiar verse. Tears dribbled as the words evoked raw emotions. A deep breath escaped slowly as she scanned the paddocks again. *This is mine. This is ours. We will make it. No matter what nature throws at us.*

She knew many Australians before them had fought the land, and in harsher climates in harder times. Farming pulsed through their veins and they were not going to be the one generation who gave up.

'Cooee! I'm home.'

She closed the little book, brushed the back of her hand across her wet cheek and went to greet her husband. As she watched him stride across the dry ground, making miniature dust storms with every step, her heart spoke the next line of Dorothea Mackellar's poem.

'A wide brown land for me.'

The Golden Bauble

A golden bauble sits in my hand
I hold it softly
for it could crush
into pieces
like my fragile heart

She accepted the birth of Christmas
showed the joy of one redeemed
her path was clear
the way absolute
life trod easy on her soul

Caring for me
she ignored expletives filling my speech
my resolute distancing from faith
made her frown with sorrowful longing
that I would someday find her God

I delighted in knowing her
connection complete
we loved; despite differences
sharing earth's blessings
becoming one

Bright flowers covered her coffin
psalms sung in praise
she wanted no mourning
for angels awaited
welcoming the believer

Habits of Christmas now face me
thoughts of celebration
recollections build
carols of the Child
echoed hope for mankind

The bauble dangles freely
from a branch of my tree
it glistens
and cheers my heart
with memories

Ruby Inheritance

Edith ran her young fingers over the decorated handle of her mother's gold spoon. As the remaining item of her family's fortune, it had become her talisman.

She tried to remember the opulent life her mother, Lady Swinbourne, had so loved. Servants, beautiful gowns, glorious banquets, bedrooms with soft pillows, libraries full of books – but all disappeared with Edith's parents' sudden death eighteen months ago. All sold. Now only a figure in a bank vault.

Edith pulled her cloak tighter around her wheezing chest. After the coughing eased, she rose from the step and returned to the humid kitchen.

'Come on, you lazy child. Get a move on,' Cook yelled. 'Sir don't want to be waitin' for his dinner.'

Edith pushed her curls under the cap and hung up her cloak. Soon she was wiping away onion-induced tears.

Once the evening meal had been served and the dishes done, Edith slipped away to her room. She removed the spoon from her pocket and touched the ruby-encrusted family crest. If she sold the spoon, she could travel to her Aunt in Scotland. There she would be welcomed. Did it matter if she had to give up her inheritance in order to be free of pernickety lawyers, demanding masters and soul-destroying days?

Determined to triumph over her father's shocking codicil on his will, Edith tucked the spoon under the pillow and made a promise to herself. She would be brave and see out the year in servitude. When her dowry was released in ten months, she could once again become self-sufficient.

The Yellow Rolls Royce

Small grains of sand forced their way under Billy's fingernails as he ran the oblong piece of wood around the make-believe racetrack.

'The winner,' he shouted. He jumped up, waved the blue block above his head. 'Zoom, zoom. Hurray!'

He squatted down on the edge of the sandpit and placed four blocks on the starting line.'This time it's your turn,' he told the yellow block.

Absorbed in his game, he didn't hear his mother calling him until she stood over him and clipped him on the back of his head.

'I've been calling you, Billy. For goodness sake, put away those silly blocks and get a move on. Your father will be home soon.'

Billy gripped the block and stood up. His mother's eyebrows were so low he could hardly see her eyes. The thumb of her right hand flicked her index fingernail and her foot tapped in time to her annoyance. He knew he would have to move quickly or her strong scrawny hand would slap his backside.

'They're not blocks, they're racing cars,' he said defiantly as he picked the coloured pieces of wood from the sand. 'Zoom, zoom. The yellow one was going to win this time.'

'I don't care who was going to win. Get your seven-year-old self inside at once.'

Billy was already moving towards the house. From the tone in her voice, he knew there wasn't any chance of playing for a few more minutes.

'Get that sand off! And stop daydreaming. You've chores to do.'

After he stood by the back door and brushed one foot against the other, he placed the blocks on the windowsill and tried to blow the sand off them. His squiggly drawings of wheels, doors and windows helped him imagine them as expensive cars.

'One day,' he said in a whisper. 'One day I'll drive a real one.'

Sandra ran all the way home from school. Pushing open the fly-wire door she started yelling, 'Mum, Mum, I'm captain. I'm captain.'

She threw her school bag on the kitchen chair and scurried up the passage. 'Mum, where are you?'

'What's all this yelling then?' Mrs Longley asked as she manoeuvred the mop and bucket from the bathroom.

Leaning against the wall, Sandra took several deep breaths. 'Mum, they made me captain.'

'Captain of what?'

'Yellow.'

'Yellow Division! My goodness, that's terrific. I know you'll do a good job.'

Sandra was good at organising.

During her tenth year she'd held a street stall from family discards, walked the neighbour's dog for some pocket money and grew cuttings from stolen pieces of geraniums.

She saved each earned coin until there was enough to deposit into a bank account, labelled 'Posh Car'.

As Sandra and Jeff, the boys' captain, held up the trophy presented to the winning team on Sports Day, her grade seven teacher said to his colleague, 'Remember her. She'll go far.'

'I'm not wearing those awful things,' nine-year-old Florette sulked. She threw an expensive turquoise dress to the floor and kicked new black shoes under her bed.

Mrs Fotheringham sighed. 'What's wrong with them? I only bought them yesterday.'

'I hate them. They'll make me look like a baby.'

'You have to wear something. And you'll have to decide soon, dear, or we'll be late.'

Florette stood in front of her mother, a patterned skirt screwed up in her hands. Her eyes were half closed with disdain. 'I don't care. If I have to sing in front of the mayor, I'm not wearing that. Or this.'

She flung several more dresses from their hangers before settling on a yellow sleeveless A-line dress.

Mrs Fotheringham picked up the discarded clothes and tried her best to remain calm. 'Florrie, dear, please hurry. Your father is waiting.

'Don't call me that, my name is Florette.' Her piercing voice came from the wardrobe as she tossed shoes aside. 'When I'm rich and famous, I'll be able to take as long as I like. My chauffeur will have to wait and the audience will, I just know they will.'

'Yes, dear, but right now you should hurry.'

July 1975

The Daily Telegraph reports the death of singing sensation Florette Fotheringham. The pop star had been on her way to a sell-out concert. The 23,000 fans were understandably shocked. Many stayed for over an hour after the announcement, watching the video of the famous singer on the big screen.

Miss Fotheringham's recently appointed chauffeur William Stenhouse, and her dedicated personal assistant, Sandra Longley, were also killed in the accident.

It is assumed the dense fog covering the notorious bend on the southbound freeway caused the collision with the semi-trailer. The Fire and Rescue Squad had to be called to enable the bodies of the victims to be released from the yellow Rolls Royce.

The Silver Box

The silver box sat on the dressing table next to the photo of Phemie's parents. She wasn't a sentimental person overall, but today was special. It was her wedding day. Her freshly painted nails clicked on the glass as she touched her mother's face with a transported kiss on the end of her finger. She gave a mental hug to her father and not for the first time, wished they could be with her. That was one wish the wishing box could never fulfil.

Only fourteen when her parents died in a car crash, Phemie's world turned upside down, and despite Aunt Freya's best efforts, she spent a year filled with resentment and tears.

On her fifteenth birthday, Aunt Freya gave her a small, decorative silver box. 'It's a wishing box, my lass. One is to write an earnest wish on a piece of paper and leave it folded in the box. Nothing too grand, mind. And be careful what you wish for.'

Phemie turned the box over in her hands and, with a less than genuine smile, said, 'It can't possibly grant wishes.' Then, relenting a little, added, 'But it's a very pretty box.'

That evening she wrote her dearest wish *I want my Mum & Dad* on a scrap of paper torn from the corner of her homework pad and placed the birthday gift next to the photo on the dresser.

Phemie also wrote *Cold Chisel* on a square of paper and waited for results. Within a week, she received a letter in the mail saying she had won a gift voucher from the local music store. 'Wow! Maybe it does work,' she exclaimed to her aunt.

That night she set her goal a little higher – *New jeans like Amy's.* Grandfather sent some belated birthday money and so a visit to the shops became a reality.

She reread her original wish and with a sad sigh placed it in the box with her next request. *New shoes for Brooke's party*. Phemie couldn't imagine how this one could be granted.

She didn't have to wait long. Mrs Hardcastle from next door called to her as she arrived home from school the next day. 'Hello, Phemie dear, have you got a moment?'

Dumping her bag at the front door, Phemie followed the neighbour inside.

'See all this stuff – my granddaughter left it behind. Would you like any of it?'

Phemie suffered a long and uninteresting story about why the reckless granddaughter came to leave her belongings behind. Seems they weren't needed on some backpacking trip. However, Phemie came away with two tops and a pair of Converse shoes.

There certainly seemed to be a pattern emerging, and Phemie decided to test the wishing box with something harder.

The school ball approached and so far no one had asked her to be his partner. Phemie chose pink perfumed notepaper and wrote, *Elliott McKenzie for my partner* and tucked it into the silver box. As she placed the lid on the box she whispered, 'Please, please. This wish, pleeease.'

Elliot, the cutest boy in school, could choose any one of the eager girls who would be thrilled to accompany him to the ball. Unfortunately for Phemie, the wishing box didn't deliver. She ended up having to ask her cousin Phillip to partner her. She cursed the wishing box so loudly Aunt Freya came to see what was wrong.

'Don't fret, little one,' she said. 'Sometimes wishes take time to come true.'

'That's a lot of good. The school ball is tomorrow.'

'Well, that's twenty-four hours away.'

'Impossible! Elliott is hardly going to dump his date for me. I might as well throw that wish away.'

'No, you mustn't.' Aunt Freya placed her hand on Phemie's arm. 'A wish is a wish. Leave it there.'

Elliott and the captain of the netball team were voted Belle and Beau of the Ball. Phemie spent most of the evening uselessly hoping she would at least get one dance with Elliott.

Young girls grow up and although the silver box remained on her dressing table, Phemie left her wishes unwritten.

She coped with life's obstacles and accepted the blessings that came her way. She married Jack Wittleby at the age of twenty-three and looked forward to settling down to family life. Jack had other ambitions and it wasn't long before he departed for his 'true calling' in deepest Africa.

Phemie ended up back with Aunt Freya. Her old bedroom became her home once more. As she unpacked her personal belongings, she came across the little silver box and nostalgically placed it next to the now faded photograph of her parents.

'Settled in, my love?' Aunt Freya asked as she brought her a hot drink.

'Thanks, Auntie. What would I do without you? I hope I'm not too much trouble.'

'Phemie, my lass, I love having you here. It's like old times.' Aunt Freya put the mug on the dresser. 'Oh, I see you still have the wishing box.'

'Yes, I'll have to start using it again,' Phemie chuckled.

'And what would you wish for now, my dear?'

Phemie frowned before saying, 'I don't know. It seems unable to grant wishes to do with the heart. Perhaps I should go for something materialistic. Diamonds, a sports car, maybe a holiday in Hawaii.' She grinned and asked, 'Do you think that would work?'

It was Aunt Freya's turn to laugh. 'One never can tell. Maybe we should try it.'

In a frivolous mood, Phemie and Freya wrote a number of unrealistic items on paper and folded the slips as small as possible.

'Oh, look!' exclaimed Aunt Freya, when she lifted the lid. 'You haven't thrown the old ones out.'

Phemie, a little embarrassed, explained, 'No, I could never throw out my first wish. It seemed as if I would be declaring the loss all over again. Elliott McKenzie, well, he stayed in there because I'd forgotten about it really. But I don't suppose I can throw him out either. It reminds me of my schooldays.'

They scrunched down their new wishes, closed the lid and retreated to the comfy sofa and a night in front of the television.

Six months later, an invitation for the tenth year school reunion turned up in Phemie's inbox. Seemed 'everyone' was going and Amy pressed her to attend.

An evening where everyone rehashed tales of their schooldays made Phemie pleased she'd attended. She kept hoping to see Elliot, but no one knew if he was expected or not.

It was nearing the end of the event when a soft touch on her arm caused her to turn around.

'Phemie? It has to be? I'm glad I recognised you. How are you? Can I get you a drink of something? Coffee perhaps.' Elliott's smile reached his eyes as he pecked her on the cheek.

She managed to stammer out a greeting and an answer in the affirmative.

They found a corner for a quiet chat. Phemie glossed over her story, and listened as Elliott told of his exploits in exotic places. He had now returned home after spending several years in Singapore with a mining consortium. By the time they finished a second cup of coffee, she had promised to see him again.

Aunt Freya gently placed a string of pearls around her niece's neck. She smiled into the mirror. 'Beautiful, you look just beautiful, my lass.'

'I couldn't be happier, Auntie. Second time lucky, I reckon.'

'Oh, definitely. You've certainly struck gold this time.'

'Just think, maybe this old silver wishing box does have some magic after all.'

'What was it you wished for?'

'Not just me! Remember how many things we wrote down. We were very indulgent.'

Phemie removed the lid and tipped the pieces of paper out of the box. She read each one as she dealt them out like cards. 'We really went for it, didn't we? And now I'll have all that and more.'

Aunt Freya nodded. 'He's a very wealthy man.'

Phemie responded quickly. 'You know it's not about the money.'

'Of course, dear, I can see love in your eyes.'

Phemie hugged her aunt. 'And I'm so glad you're going to come and live with us.'

'Mm, in a little while perhaps.'

Aunt Freya noticed some pieces hadn't fallen from the box and picked them out.

'Not that one, leave my original wish in there, please, Auntie.'

'There's two pieces. What's this one? It's pink.' She unfolded the piece of paper and laughed so much her voice caught, but managed to say, 'Well, well, took it's time.'

Phemie accepted the slip from her aunt's outstretched hand. She, too, laughed heartily. The piece of pink paper revealed the wish she had written so many years ago – *Elliott McKenzie for my partner.*

Colour Me Black

The malignant hue reflects from the mirror
Covers me
Envelopes perception of my day

I see only discouragement
Feel only discontent

Carrying pain with every step
I know no future without it

Colour me black today
For my world is monochrome
And I grieve hope

Golden Cage

Sheila's bank account showed $10.20. How could she pay next week's rent? After working for only three months in an accountancy firm, she'd been made redundant – no payout.

The young woman at Centrelink rolled her eyes as she told Sheila she'd have to wait six weeks for funds.

'What do I do in the meantime? I have to eat, pay the rent.'

'Ring your parents?'

The non-helpful advice had Sheila struggling for control. 'Nup, none of those.'

'Friends?'

'Can't ask them.'

The young women leaned across the desk, glanced left and right before whispering. 'My friend works for that pub in Kewmount. It's… well, you know. You're pretty enough. They'll give you a job. Try them.'

'You'll have to change your name,' the entertainment manager of the Kewmount Hotel said. 'What about Lolita? Or Desiree? Roxi?'

His leer made her squirm. Sheila thought she was applying for a job in the office, but things had turned out differently after the manager liked what he saw. Roxi? Why not, thought Shelia. Better pay. And… better than living on the streets.

'You can start with Tuesdays. Not a big crowd, but depending how good you are, maybe we'll slot you in on Saturday arvo as well.'

With Roxi's promotion, the birdcages are once again empty on Tuesdays. Shelia bumps and grinds her way inside the large golden birdcage on Saturday evenings – the most lucrative of all the shows at the salubrious Kewmount Hotel.

White Car Ambush

Honestly, I really didn't think it would come to this. I was positive my son would see sense.

She, the excessively buxom, heavily made-up tart, wormed her way into his affections with that wanton smile and those 'come hither' eyes. Enough to make me sick. But Kieran, and for that matter my husband Walter, couldn't see past the brassy hair and the figure of a tramp.

I mean, what sort of name is Blythe? Sounds like a wind too lazy to do its own work. Well, it suits her. I certainly got that impression when she visited. She just sat there on my expensive couch pretending to pull down an excuse for a skirt over her knees. Wally danced around, offering her our best sherry and then, when she refused that, he dug out the top-shelf Scotch. I mean, there was no need for alcohol when I had made such an effort to prepare afternoon tea.

She, this lithe Blythe, was the latest girlfriend of my one and only son, so I pulled out all the stops. I rinsed my best Wedgwood tea set. I purchased the lamingtons only this morning. When I offered her cream, she looked me up and down and said that it wasn't good for one's figure. Well, I never! I had my best Target dress on, which draped nicely over my generous curves. Wally had said I looked nice, but I hesitate to divulge the theatrics he created when we opened the front door to long legs protruding from a wisp of a dress.

As the months went by, I had to put up with many similar visits. Wally continued to be besotted by Blythe. I quickly realised she was only after Kieran's inheritance. She ogled the two Picasso prints – a real bargain from the local Bring and Buy, and then she asked how long it had taken to collect all my crystal ornaments. I could tell from her raised eyebrows she was ticking off how much they were worth.

Kieran turned up on one such visit driving a new BMW sports car. He said something about it being a gift from Blythe in return for the engagement ring. Well, I didn't believe that for a moment. Where would a common person like her get so much money? Her father is only a truck driver. She works at some sort of boutique in Nedlands – probably in the back room.

The final straw came when they announced the wedding date. I won't bore you with the details, but the fuss, my goodness, it really was too much.

Walter and I trimmed our side of the list to twenty-five to help keep expenses down, but they invited two hundred guests to partake of drinks at the restaurant in Kings Park. Then, before the reception, back in the same restaurant, we had to traipse off across the lawn and put up with a garden wedding. I really don't see how one can feel married unless blessed by the church.

I won't tell you what I think of spending all that money on flowers to decorate a rotunda for twenty minutes, and then there's the quintet of violins. Poor Kieran will have to get another job to cover the exorbitant costs.

We did offer to help pay for the wedding, but when the over-the-top plans surfaced I made it clear we could only do so much. Just between you and me, I was rather glad when they refused our one-thousand-dollar offer. Now Walter and I can have a holiday in Albany and get over the thought of having to put up with Blythe as a daughter-in-law.

Kieran insists Blythe's father is paying for it all. Something about a national fleet of trucks. It doesn't matter how many trucks – one is still just a *truck driver*.

Kieran could have done so much better. All those expensive school fees – he did look rather handsome in the uniform. And, when he learned to drive, we gave him the Barina instead of trading it for our updated Mazda. Oh well, one can only try and help.

So now I'm standing here waiting for the bride. I used some of the unwanted money to purchase a stunning outfit. It was just what I was after – a pale mauve three-piece. It will do me for best for quite a while, so the fifty dollars was well spent.

Just a minute, what in the name of heavens is that coming up the road? Maybe the tasteless convoy will drive right on past us. Oh no, they've stopped and Miss Blythe is getting out. We are being ambushed by white limousines. Six of them! And full of tarted-up females and silly little girls. Oh dear, children never do go well at weddings.

I realise everyone doesn't have my taste and, for that matter, my class. Truly I shall be the laughing stock of my relatives. My sisters Judith and Penelope have already asked to be introduced to Kieran's new in-laws. What am I to do? I hope they won't make a fuss over having to drink foreign wine – Dom Pierre Champagne…or some French name, so I'm told. I've seen the menu and the entrée has something called truffles with other things any decent person wouldn't want to eat. They wouldn't listen to me – prawn cocktails would have been more palatable. Oh, the embarrassment of it all.

You will have to excuse me; I have to take my place at the front. Despite all the excessive frippery they insisted on, I have an important part to play. I'm the mother of the groom and the wedding can't go on without me.

Braver

It's lifeless. The greens are too pale. The blues…insipid. Jake grimaces, steps back and analyses his painting again. Yep, too much wash. Maybe I'd better let it dry.

He wipes his hands on a stained piece of cloth, drinks greedily from a can and walks down a path to the edge of the river.

While he considers if he'll continue the struggle or pack up and go home, he watches people glancing at his unfinished painting. One looks around, probably expecting the artist to appear. A child touches the wet paint. Her mother won't be pleased with the verdant green now spread across the white T-shirt.

Time to get back to it, he thinks, and eases himself to his feet. As he ambles across the park, an elderly woman approaches his easel. She leans heavily on her walking stick and peers closely at his work. He stops and waits.

She turns, glances at people close by with a questioning raised eyebrow, then picks up a brush, wriggles it through the murky jar of water and shakes the excess across the grass.

Jake leans against a tree. His frown deepens as intrigue builds.

The woman dabs at the palette and then lays the colour carefully in one of the white spaces. She stretches forward and blows, attempting to dry the first application.

She works slowly, dipping the brush into different hues, considering each combination.

Jake steps closer.

The woman looks up and spots him. 'Oh, hi, is this yours?' she asks.

Nodding slowly, he examines the picture.

'I couldn't resist.' She tips her head sideways, purses her lips with an unspoken apology. 'It needed some help.'

He forces a smile at her and then returns to his inspection. Her bright colours seem to admonish his anaemic attempt.

'That's great,' he says. 'You've certainly made an improvement.' His painting has sprung to life.

'Look, young man.' She waves the cobalt-blue-filled brush at him. 'You've got to be braver.'

He nods again. 'Mm, yes. Maybe that's what I've been doing wrong.' His eyes narrow as he inspects a variety of colours splattering across the foreground. 'Your colour choices are exceptional.'

Her left cheek has a crimson smudge and her chin displays a spot of ochre. She lifts her head and grins. 'You know, I haven't had this much fun in ages.' Using the end of the paintbrush, she flicks a leaf from his shoulder. 'Haven't picked up my paintbrushes in ages. Couldn't even see a reason to leave the house some days.'

Jake wonders how one could become insular when the world demands so much. Remembering her hesitant steps and her bent back, he realises not everyone races through life like he does. Unrelenting ambition has taken its toll. Long working hours leave no time for relaxation. In fact, time spent with this diversion is rare. No wonder he's been unable to recreate the character of the paperbarks and the shadows falling across the water.

He notices her age-spotted hand as she rinses the brush and places it across the top of the water jar. 'Well,' he says, 'you should definitely paint more often.' Jake's playful chuckle makes his eyes sparkle. 'Actually, you should get out more. You know…be braver.'

Now, two easels stand in the park on Sundays. One is lower, allowing the artist to be seated.

Absence of a Rainbow

What if the rainbow colours refused to join in the promise
When the gentle light caressed the rain

The blue would fill a river
Splash between the reeds
Orange would bounce off sun's rays
The colour drunk in by the glow
Twirls of glee would see indigo dance
Peaking between thunderclouds
Dodging the lightening that encased the yellow
Fields of wind-blown young crops beckons
A ribbon of creeping green
Pretty heads of pansies
Curtsy with velvet skirts
Enfolded by violet sparkles straight from the sky

Each colour brings expansion in its own way
Nature would oblige
But the joy of that glorious vision
That spans the earth
That brings forth a gasp of beauty
Must be

Red, yellow must start the arc

With orange, green and blue

Bound alongside indigo and violet

For mere mortals eyes

The oath of a god that shows magnificence

Filling a dewy horizon

In the wonderful refraction

Of a rainbow

Crimson Scarf

Out of eyes of blue came softness from the soul
Bringing a question from the passer-by
The crimson scarf, worn with a grief-filled pride
Bringing a question from the passer-by
Sadness reflected from every pose
Tiredness showed with every breath
The passer-by could only question

Huddled against the back of the bus, Alice fiddled with the buttons on her grubby cardigan. The bags at her feet meant she constantly shuffled to keep the items from spilling onto the floor. Wispy portions of hair dangled around her face hiding a demanding amount of eye make-up.

At each stop, this traveller glanced urgently up and down the pavement as if expecting someone. Broad bands of rings covered several fingers. Her hands once again tugged at her clothes. The mere quantity of white stones made one imagine they weren't diamonds even though they sparkled as the sun slashed through the moving windows. The beads around her age-creased neck hung down to her waist, accompanied by a beautiful red silk scarf. Occasionally, the two life-worn hands would caress the scarf. A slow smile and softening of the eyes, which showed the sentimentality of her soul, were visible to other passengers.

Alice was making her daily trip to the cemetery to visit Jacob and Susan. Today the bus was crowded and as it turned sharply around the corners, Alice jerked out of her reverie.

A flash of golden hair, spotted at a bus stop, made her heart leap, but in an instant grief overwhelmed her again – for it could not be her daughter.

If only Susan were still here, Alice's heart cried. Susan would cheer me. Susan would have a smile for everyone. I would be happy. Her daughter would have caressed the crimson scarf and spoke of the father she loved.

Susan had called it her scarf. 'One day it'll be mine, Mum,' she said with a twinkle in her eyes.

The scarf had been Jacob's last gift to Alice, for he knew his time to die was near. Jacob had pressed money into a nurse's hand with instructions to 'buy something nice for my wife'.

When Alice and Susan visited, they wore their bravest face, as tears were just an emotion away. It had been a melancholy day with love flooding the hospital room. Barely able to conjure up enough strength to talk, Jacob pointed to the package at the foot of the bed and asked Alice to keep it close. *Think of me.* Then he held their hands and called them his favourite girls for the last time.

Alice fell in love with the gift immediately. It was not her usual colour choice, but the luxurious feel of the silk was unbelievably perfect. As she caressed the scarf that day, she knew it would always remind her of Jacob, for it was the colour of love.

Mother and daughter would visit Jacob's grave on Susan's day off each week. Alice always wore her crimson scarf. They would sit on the grass and chat about him as if he were still there. They were able to express their sorrow easily while they recounted stories of their life as a family. Their hearts would lift and they felt a special closeness.

With the days passing slowly, the absence of Jacob became bearable. They would laugh together and they would cry together. The trip home was always silent. The subsequent grind of normality became difficult for Alice.

It was on one of these occasions, while they were sitting on the grass that Susan said how much she liked her mother's scarf.

Alice promised the crimson scarf would be part of her legacy. 'It will be yours, Susan,' she assured her daughter again.

On a fateful night of darkness, tragedy took Susan's life in an instant.

The phone call turned Alice's life into a blur. They said they were sorry. They said she had to come to the mortuary. They said someone would look after her.

As she performed the perfunctory duty of identifying the body, Alice found she couldn't take her eyes from her daughter's hair. Hair, damp and twisted, far beyond its usual beauty, strangled Alice's life force.

The broken body brought unrepairable damage to Alice's soul. She left the hospital engulfed in fog. Every action became unreal.

In days after the second loss, Alice sat on the grass by herself and whimpered. She was supposed to be lying next to Jacob – not Susan.

She felt cheated and the grieving shell of a person that was Alice couldn't see a life beyond the daily habit of visiting the cemetery. For many months now, it was her only reason for getting up in the morning. The buying of flowers was all she could now do for her husband and daughter.

The bus trip home, as the sun was sinking, was tiring and she longed for the comfort of her loved ones. Alice placed a shaky hand at the empty space around her neck.

Passers-by in the cemetery noticed a shock of crimson fluttering in the breeze. Someone had tucked the corner of a well-worn scarf under the heavy stone vase on the flower-strewn grave.

In the softness of a beautiful autumn morning, when the leaves were beginning to fall, Alice's soul soared beyond grief into the light.

Spanish Olive

Scott panicked. Elise was due to fly in this evening and he still hadn't fulfilled his promise.

Scott had the vague notion he was expected to be as excited about Sunday's lunch as his girlfriend, but that was far from the truth. He always felt out of his depth in the company of the flight attendants as they talked about far-flung places recently visited. Places where he hadn't even thought of going. It was embarrassing to listen to them denigrate travellers, and laugh over their exploitations of the first-class passengers. Elise assured him it was harmless fun, but the repetitive nature of their anecdotes made him think otherwise.

He had met Elise during a flight when he travelled business class at the insistence of a wealthy client. She had been charming, and casually dropped her phone number into his lap while asking him to prepare for landing.

The following twelve months had been stormy. Elise wouldn't acknowledge their limited budget, constantly spending more than he could afford. After moving in to his small apartment in a wealthy part of town, she accused him of hiding his finances, and making her battle on her lowly wage. However, the shoe was on the other foot.

He had put the deposit on the tumbled-down apartment after receiving a bonus and it had taken him two years to turn it into the glamorous place it was today. His pay packet hardly matched the take-home pay of an international flight attendant, who also received generous tips from adoring passengers.

During their latest argument over her need to impress her friends, Elise insisted he paint the dining room in readiness for Sunday lunch with her friends and their partners. She expected him to have time while she was walking the aisle in first class on the return flight from Rome.

So here he was standing at the paint counter, five minutes before closing time, waving Elise's paint sample at a less than helpful assistant. Another customer was being served with her tin of paint, when she rushed away to find some forgotten item. Suddenly Scott realised he would need some masking tape and, leaving his paint can to bounce around on the mixer, ran back up row 6 and grasped at the first roll within reach. In a gait that resembled an injured animal, he reached the paint counter and grabbed at the completed paint can. He apologised to the service assistant, and even more profusely to the dark-haired lady who was returning to the counter as well.

As he punched in his pin number for an impatient checkout operator, he mentally ticked off the things needed to be done to achieve what now seemed impossible. *Move the furniture, um, must make sure I cover the carpet properly. What else? What else?*

'Sorry!' he mouthed to the driver of a car he almost stepped out in front of. Relieved of the pressure of the dash to complete his purchases, he began to relax on his way home. 'Won't take long,' he told his image as he glanced into the rear-view mirror.

After he moved the heavy furniture, he rewarded his hard work with a cold beer.

'Ah, that's better,' he said as he sat on the floor in the empty room with his back against a decorator's nightmare of an orange wall. 'Right, let's see. Masking tape next.'

Scott eased to his feet, and in between sipping the refreshing ale, commenced the onerous task of placing the tape around the two doorways and the window.

Let's get this done. One coat and then I'll have something to eat, then second coat after that.

He released the lid of the paint tin. 'What the…!'

He peered at the side of the can, which read 'Base coat white'. He flipped over the lid, and cursed as his fingers slipped into the fresh paint. The bad handwriting on the lid revealed the reason for his confusion.

'Spanish Olive? Can't be! What happened to Linen Beige?' Scott sank to the floor with the wet lid sitting on his lap. He sat frozen.

He went through his actions at the paint shop. *Gave the bloke the sample slip, saw him tint the paint, then it was put into the mixing machine.*

'Oh, bugger!' he said. 'The other customer.' *I must have grabbed her paint. Now what?*

The clock, once hanging on the dining room wall, but now balancing precariously on the top of fridge, said ten-past eight. Elise was due home at 7 o'clock the next morning.

'I can't leave the room like this,' he told Elise's choice of modern art.

Two coats of paint later, Scott rather like the finished product. Spanish Olive looked good with the beige leather chairs and the glass table. He replaced the beige curtains, beige dresser and the chrome clock. Once he'd hung the bold artwork, satisfaction was complete.

'Ah, but will Elise Drummond like it? That is the burning question.'

The answer was predictable.

'How can you do this to me?' she yelled, five minutes after dumping her Louis Vuitton cases in the hall for Scott to deal with.

'I rather like it.'

'It's completely hideous. You promised to do as I asked. Linen Beige, it was supposed to be. Not some hideous olive oil.'

'Spanish Olive, and it breaks up all the beige.'

'Well, Spanish Olive or not, it has to go. You have three hours before they all arrive. Surely that stupid paint place is open today.'

The argument went on for some time, and in the end Elise used her mobile and arranged to meet her friends at Antonio's-on-Swan. Scott refused to remove the Spanish Olive, and to accompany her to lunch.

Two days later, she moved out.

The following Saturday, as he pulled into the shared parking bays at the rear of the group of units, he noticed a young lady who looked vaguely familiar. Probably one of the new tenants, he thought. But I'm sure I've I seen her somewhere else.

As they walked towards the stairs, and prompted by the paint can she carried, he asked, 'Hello. Busy painting?'

'Yep. Second time lucky.'

'Second time? What happened the first time? Someone not like the colour?' He brushed away the memory of the argument over Linen Beige.

'You wouldn't believe it. I came home with someone else's paint. It was rather a boring colour. Been busy, so it took until today to swap it.'

'Was it Spanish Olive you were after?'

She stopped walking and frowned at him. 'Yes, it was actually. That was an awfully clever guess or are you a particularly good psychic?'

Scott introduced himself to Remi after they both stopped laughing over the story of the misplaced Linen Beige.

They shared coffee among drop sheets and painting implements. Scott thought the least he could do was to help use the Spanish Olive for its original purpose.

Gold

I never found the pot of gold
The one at the end of the rainbow
I reached out at the colours
    towards:

        the red; burning memories into forever
        orange, tempting
        yellow, brighter than joy itself
        blessed blue
        calming green
        but
        indigo, darker than my darkest days
        and
        violet, hinting at something new

No, I've never touched a rainbow
Never found that pot of gold

Far more precious
I found you
And accepted a band of gold

Rainbowed Heart

Marjorie stabbed at a crystal with her walking stick. 'Stupid thing,' she said as she plopped down into the large swivel chair next to the window.

The crystal swung unhappily on its fishing line and bumped into the tiny blue bell which tinkled as it hit the adjacent piece of coloured glass.

Turning her back on the sunlight and the window adornments, Marjorie straightened her skirt and waited.

Her daughter called in on her way home from work every Thursday and as far as Marjorie was concerned, Belinda was an officious busybody who wanted to know everything. Marjorie couldn't stand all the questions. Have you enough food? Do you need any more clothes? And she was always intruding into her finances. Anyone would think she couldn't look after her own affairs.

Any minute now and her daughter would push open the door and rush in, filling the room with her own importance. She would bring some delicacy from a fancy city gourmet café, expecting her mother to be delighted with a titbit, which was supposed to make up for the inconvenience of putting on something 'decent' and getting out the best cups and saucers.

'Hello, Mum. How are you?' There she was now, her high heels clacking across the tiles as she came into the room. 'Brought you some stuffed figs. I know you like figs.'

'Figs? I only like fresh figs.' Marjorie remembered the tree covering the front of the house she and James had first lived in.

Belinda kissed her on the cheek. 'I've brought you something… well, someone…else, too. Say hello to my mother, Tara. Mum, this is Tara. Tara, this is Mrs Lonegan.'

'Hi, Mrs Lonegan. What a lovely window.'

A child? Where did she get a child from? Stolen from a crowded train?

'Tara – what sort of name is that?'

'Don't be rude, Mother.'

'You'll have to get another cup. Don't get a good one. Not for a child. Get a glass. From the everyday cupboard.' Marjorie pointed her walking stick at Tara. 'Where did you get such a child?'

Belinda wanted to snap back at her mother. There was no need for her to be so crotchety, but making time to visit was important, even though she felt unwelcome. She was the state manager of a successful clothing manufacturer, self-reliant and content, but it wasn't enough for her mother – because Belinda remained single at forty-five. Her mother wasn't happy unless she was comparing Belinda to her younger sister – a mother to a batch of rough-and-ready boys.

But, dutifully, Belinda did as she was told and chose an everyday glass and poured Tara some pineapple juice.

'Tara's mother is a friend of mine. She's in hospital for a couple of days. Tara's staying with me until Sunday.'

'No father then? What about your *important* job? How come you can take time off?'

Belinda would have explained it was possible these days to communicate with the office without leaving home, and that Tara's father worked on the mines, his roster not allowing for a quick trip home, but her mother wouldn't have listened.

'The crystals are very pretty, Mrs Lonegan.'

'If you say so,' Marjorie said. 'I don't look at them much.'

'You should.' Tara pointed to a small crystal ball. 'See how the sun shines through it.'

'Can't really be bothered.'

'Look. Look at the pretty rainbow on your wall.'

'Drink your juice, child.'

'Mrs Lonegan, where did you get them all from?' Tara asked.

'Can't remember.'

'What about this one shaped like a heart? Was it from someone special?'

'Drink your juice, child.'

When Belinda and Tara left, Marjorie remained in her chair, her back to the window.

She dozed for a while and awoke feeling melancholy. Pushing her stick into the floor, she swung round and faced the window. The crystals used to give her pleasure, but it was a while since she'd appreciated the twinkling rainbows scattering across the room on a sunny winter's day. Handling the heart-shaped one, she sighed and reminisced.

James and she had been delighted when Belinda was born: a dark-eyed beauty with demanding lungs, and squirming arms and legs.

When they arrived home, James presented her with the crystal. 'To sparkle forever like our daughter.'

He had been right. Belinda delighted everyone with her vivacious innocence, which grew into elegant confidence. Their second child, Andrea, had mousy brown hair and laughing blue eyes like her father, a reticent child transformed when motherhood was thrust upon her – four children in seven years.

Marjorie couldn't believe Belinda didn't want children; didn't want to be a home-body.

As she let the crystal go, it swung back and forth, blinking at Marjorie, sending red, yellow, blue across the room. When indigo fell on the wall, Marjorie eased into a standing position and struck the hanging ornaments with her walking stick.

Two hurtled to the floor. The bell bounced three times before falling silent. She watched the shattered pieces as they tumbled together making patterned shards on the dark tiles. The heart-shaped one bounced on the twine before it too broke free and landed near her foot. She gasped. Her stomach flipped and her hand went to her mouth.

Then Marjorie golf-putted the crystal, sending it under the cabinet. She sighed and said, 'Sentimental old fool.'

Colour of Courage

Speckled spots of sunlight peek through the grapevine and dance on her auburn hair. I hope she'll turn – I want to smile, nod, acknowledge how delightful it is to be enjoying this moment.

She sits on the edge of her chair, shoulders forced towards her ears. I purse my lips as I lean to the left and try to see her face. She picks up her handbag, moves as if to stand, then drops her bag on the table and wriggles back into the wrought iron chair. Her hands shake as she picks up the coffee cup. She sips tentatively.

The waiter's footsteps disturb my observation. 'Your coffee, sir.'

He stumbles on uneven bricks. The cup rattles in the saucer. The young lady leaps to her feet. I straighten my back. He regains his balance. She sits down again and wraps her arms around her body. Coffee dribbles down my cup.

I say, 'That was close.'

He apologises and dabs at the small spill.

After the waiter returns to the kitchen, I look at the young lady again. She tugs at her tied-back hair. I taste the thick black coffee. Her frown deepens as she runs her forefinger across her upper arm. A tear creeps from the corner of her eye. I ponder.

She turns towards me.

I ask if she is okay.

'Yes,' she says, 'but today is the first time I've worn this dress.'

I tell her the dress is a lovely colour.

She says, 'It's sleeveless.'

I add that she should wear it more often. She lowers her head. I raise my eyebrows.

'It takes courage,' she says.

I don't know what she means. Not until she stands, gathers her things, and walks past me. The freckled skin on her left arm is interrupted by scars. Different shades of puckered pink mingle with healing pale patches.

I tell her the dress suits her perfectly. She nods and thanks me. The waiter appears and shows her to the door.

I hope she'll be back. In her sleeveless dress. With her glorious hair loose. With a smile for me.

Observation

67

Smoke shot from between scarlet lips. The wafting air caught the softening greyness and it drifted lazily upwards.

A conundrum of a woman sat under a broad-leafed tree. Her Prada handbag sat on Target slacks and the Hermes scarf did its best to hide the ageing skin beneath it. The Audrey-Hepburn-type cigarette holder wobbled as it clunked against six fashionably enormous rings. Her left thumbnail had been bitten down to the quick.

She sucked in. She forced the smoke out. Her manicured brows dipped over ink-black lashes. She spat the last of the smoke from her mouth and stood up.

Her handbag fell from her knees and landed on her mud-soaked boots. A mobile phone and a sparkly glasses case tumbled out as the bag settled onto the footpath. She cursed, but didn't retrieve them.

This time, she drew back slowly, closing her eyes and savouring the experience. A hint of a cough preceded the slow exit of smoke. It caressed her puckered mouth, curled around her nose and drifted over her forehead. When the last of the smoke became absorbed in the cool air, she coughed heartily, wiped the last of her lipstick off with the back of her hand, picked up her possessions and stalked away.

By Darkened Shore

Carrie drove into a small town on the edge of Lake Tamarisk distracted by thoughts of the continuing argument with her mother. The gears crunched as she forced her foot onto the clutch a moment too late.

'Damn!'

She wiped away tears that had dribbled out for much of the journey and eased the two-door Mercedes Benz into a parking space outside the Bon Ami Café.

'If I find a good friend in this miserable place, it'll be a miracle,' Carrie said as she slung the car door shut.

She avoided damaging the heels of her expensive shoes by tiptoeing up the stone path. Pushing aside the plastic strips covering the doorway, she stepped into a brightly lit room. Lifting her skirt to stop it touching the black and white tiles, she strode towards the counter. Carrie brushed her fingers across her face which shifted her mascara from where it had run onto her cheek to beneath her nose, making a semblance of a moustache.

The hovering waitress looked Carrie over with amusement. A nearby customer raised his eyebrows, offered a wry smile, then recommended eating.

From behind the counter, Patty tried to look somewhere else except at the black streak. 'Can I help you?'

'I hope so. I didn't stop at this town for the good of my health,' Carrie replied.

Patty's eyebrows danced as she took a moment to respond politely. 'Do you want to order something? You can order off the board for takeaway or sit down and we'll take your order when you're ready.'

'I'll sit.'

The menu revealed basic fare and Carrie ordered strong black coffee along with a chicken and salad sandwich.

'Anything else?' Patty asked as she checked the order.

'No thanks.' Carrie propped the menu between the salt and pepper shakers, and as Patty turned to go, mumbled, 'Not unless you know a mansion to rent and a psychiatrist to go with it.'

The sadness in the sarcastic comment caused Patty to hesitate before she returned to the kitchen.

Commenting on the regularity of odd people who came their way, Patty indicated the young woman sitting near the window. 'Take a look at table sixteen, Bert. I'd say this one's a bit richer than the usual odd ones coming through here. Seems to be in a spot of bother.'

'As long as they pay for their food, I don't care what their problems are,' Bert said as he glanced through the half-opened door. He agreed she looked more 'dressed up' than the locals, but returned to the stove and flipped the bacon over.

Patty peered through the bifold doors at the customer. The hunched-over figure was making circles with a manicured finger in the spilt salt. Dark brown trusses hid most of her face, but bare lips quivered below the accidental moustache. Patty withdrew from witnessing someone else's burden.

'Here you go. You can pay when you've finished.' Patty placed the plate on the table.

'Thanks, but take the money now or I might forget later.'

'You sure?'

'Yes, and keep the change. Won't miss it.'

After retreating to the cash register, Patty watched the customer play with her food. The woman chose a piece of chicken and chewed with such deliberation Patty wondered if it was tough. Then she rearranged the remainder of the sandwich in a neat pile on the serviette. However, after a testing sip, she finished the coffee in one tip of the mug.

Bert had to yell at Patty to attend to the meals queuing up for other customers. She responded quickly, but her frown deepened. She knew a troubled soul when it was in front of her.

'Can I get you anything else?' Patty asked, offering more coffee.

'Does it look like I need anything else?' came back lazy words without anger.

Patty slipped onto the chair opposite and spoke softly, 'Is there anything I can do?'

Carrie lifted her streaky face and looked at the person who had spoken kindly to her. It's a kind face, thought Carrie. 'Perhaps. I was going further on, but after stopping I've lost enthusiasm. What's the best option for just a night or two? Something close.'

'Sorry. There's nothing in town. Not even a motel. It really is a small town. What you see in the main street is it, really.'

'Well, that's just my luck. Trust me to bomb out in a one-horse town.'

Patty ignored the half-hearted insult and asked, 'Do you want another coffee? I could get you a nice hot one.'

A slight smile made the troubled eyes soften. 'Sure, that'll prolong any decision for a while.'

Patty went through to the kitchen and started making fresh coffee. 'Bert, know of anywhere to stay around here?'

'You thinking of leaving Jim?' Bert already knew the answer.

Patty chuckled. 'Yeah, right. No, there's a young woman outside who's looking for somewhere for a couple of nights. I can't think of anything.'

'In all my fifty years in this town, the only place to stay is with people you know.'

'Damn, it looks like she could do with some help.'

Banging the greasy egg slicer on the side of the hotplate, Bert said, 'Hang on, what about my old boat shed? I mean, it's rather run-down, but it has a bathroom and a kitchen sink. If she's desperate, it would do for a couple of nights.'

'You're a whizz, Bert. She seemed pretty beat, so she might go for it. Can I show her where it is?'

'Sure. You like gathering lost kittens, don't you, Patty? The keys are hanging in the meter box. Don't be long. We have work to do, you know.'

Patty gave her boss a hug and disappeared out the swinging doors. She found Carrie sitting in her car, leaning over the steering wheel, trying to get the key in the ignition. Not able to achieve that simple task, she threw the key out the window and they landed at Patty's feet.

'Useless! Useless!' Carrie screamed as she beat her fists on the dashboard. Then lowered her head and sobbed quietly, with intermittent half-audible expletives.

Left-over salad bounced out of the serviette and fell onto the floor.

Patty retrieved the keys and stood in front of the open window. She placed a soft touch on the driver's shoulder and without speaking held her hand there until the crying eased. 'Look, I'm sure I don't want to interfere, but it looks like you need some help. What can I do?' Patty offered Carrie a clean tissue.

When Carrie lifted her face from the steering wheel, Patty noticed the torrent of tears had washed away the moustache. Carrie's brown eyes were half-closed and her lipstick-smudged mouth drooped in an effort to form words.

'I'm sorry you had to see that. Everything's gone wrong. I just wanted to get away. I don't seem capable of going any further.'

Leaning against the car, Patty said, 'It's okay, everyone has a bad day now and again.'

'I suppose,' Carrie said. She wiped away the last of her lipstick as she checked her face in the mirror. 'I guess I could sleep in my car if you could spare a driveway.'

Patty pointed to the last speck of mascara on Carrie's cheek. 'Missed a bit.' She forced a smile. 'Look, if you really want to stay, I have a better idea than sleeping in your car. Can you drive a little way? If you follow me, I'll show you somewhere you could stay.'

Carrie flicked her over-abundance of hair from her face and brightened slightly. 'Really? I thought you said there was no motel. I don't mind if it's not a four-star.'

Amid gentle laughter, Patty explained it was far from any star, but Bert's boat shed would give her a roof over her head for a few nights.

Once at the boat shed, Patty retrieved the all too conspicuous key and led Carrie through the large empty boat storage area to the small living quarters at the side of the building.

'Bert used to have lots of boats here,' Patty explained. 'Now there's just the one outside that's rotted where he left it. He used to take people out on the lake for sightseeing trips and a spot of fishing. Tourists still stop to see if they can go out on the lake, but Bert's creaky bones put paid to all that.'

The facilities might have been adequate for a fishing stopover but they caused a grimace from Carrie. However, she knew she would have to accept this offer or travel a considerable distance to the next town; something she didn't want to do. She brought in her small case and was about to query the availability of food stocks.

Patty spoke first. 'Look, there aren't many supplies. Probably just some coffee, tea and sugar if the mice haven't got it. I could go back to town and bring some supplies for you.'

'I couldn't expect that, you've already done more than enough. Is there a supermarket in town?'

'One of sorts. You can get practically anything there if you aren't fussy.'

Carrie pulled out her mobile. 'Do they deliver?'

'Probably, but make a list and I'll drop it in on my way back. Young Jason will bring it out to you. You could come into the café for dinner.'

Shaking her head, Carrie said, 'No, I came looking for solitude. If you don't mind, I really need to be by myself.'

Once Patty left, Carrie checked out the room. She found a stretcher bed with grey blankets folded neatly under two pillows. Dust covered the pile of magazines on the chest of drawers, the uneven-legged coffee table and the kitchen bench. The bathroom revealed the lack of recent attention. The tap rasped its way into offering some water, which Carrie forced around the basin. She was horrified at the sight of her image that bounced out of the mirror, and dabbed cold water over her face.

Not able to convince herself she was happy with her surroundings, she walked past the run-down boat and into the sunshine. Water lapped carelessly over a pebbly beach a few metres from the boat shed. The size of the lake, the movement of the gentle waves and the quietness of the place surprised her. She stood still and absorbed the view. Wasn't she used to the best of everything? Hadn't she seen most of the exotic places in the world? She certainly could travel to all the wonders of the world by merely making a phone call, but here she was, entranced by this simple scenery.

Carrie sat on the small jetty for three hours enjoying the inactivity. When Jason pulled up with her groceries, she felt annoyed she had to expend energy for everyday matters. Then, with a can of cola in her hand, she returned to the end of the jetty and watched the sun disappear behind the tall trees.

In the darkness, she struggled to find her way across the stones back to the door. She ignored the supplies scattered across the small bench, sat down and slumped against the cushion on the couch. With nothing to entice her to move, she sat listening to the absence of noise. The silence made her face the questions that had caused her to leave her home in a hurry. Why aren't I good enough? Why aren't I old enough? She sobbed the last question, 'What can I do?'

Drawn back to the jetty, and, with a little light as the moon peeped out from the clouds like a shy child, Carrie sat with her legs crossed under the many folds of her skirt until they demanded circulation. Her high-fashion shoes clung precariously as she dropped her legs over the edge.

At five a.m. the sun shot threads of light through the trees. Carrie had been shivering for the last hour but otherwise hadn't moved. She had hitched her skirt up around her shoulders as a shawl while one shoe had finally dropped into the dark depths. Now she forced herself into a standing position and limped back to the boat shed.

The prickly blanket disgusted Carrie; she could see no comfort in the lumpy pillow and despised the fact there were no crisp laundered sheets. She didn't bother to change. She was sure she wouldn't sleep.

Loud knocking woke her, and Carrie momentarily wondered where she was.

'Hi there, feeling better?' Patty asked tentatively as she slowly opened the unlocked door. Then as her eyes got accustomed to the shadowy room, she squinted at Carrie. 'Are you okay?'

'Yes. Well, not really, but what do you expect?'

Patty looked at Carrie. It was obvious she'd slept in her clothes, but it was four o'clock in the afternoon! Carrie was bare-footed and her hair a tangled disaster.

Patty released an esky from her grip. 'I don't expect anything. What is it that you expect?'

Dark curls cascaded over her face as Carrie dropped her head. After an awkward silence, she lifted haunted eyes and looked at Patty. 'Sorry. Not quite the obligatory nice person today.' She folded her arms defensively around her slim frame and looked down at her feet.

'I've brought you an esky and ice blocks. Thought you might like somewhere to keep the milk fresh. I won't stay, but I suggest you take a shower. Here's a clean towel. Maybe come in to the café for something to eat.'

When there was no response, Patty placed the towel on the esky, turned and left. She was nearly to her car before she heard 'Thank you' uttered as Carrie closed the door softly.

Carrie took the well-meaning advice and showered. With a change of clothes and her wet hair tied securely, she headed for the kitchen area.

'Mm, I haven't had baked beans for ages, pity there isn't pecorino and basil to go with them.'

After eating half the warmed beans, she wandered down to the lake, walking for some time before settling down on the jetty and waiting. The darkness slowly slipped around her; encasing her emotions within her jumbled thoughts.

She was sure her father had wanted her to take over the family business. Why else had he trained her all those years? Those laborious days of putting up with the heat of the factory, and tedious hours spent over the finances of the company. All those times when she wanted to walk down the boulevards of Paris instead of being stuck in those business meetings; surely it wasn't all for nothing. She thumped the wooden planks repeatedly until she felt pain.

Water sprayed onto her face and shook her out of the downward spiral. She looked up into the face of the moon and felt the smallness of her being. Her feet sloshed in the cold waves and her anger eased. The stillness of the night was calming and Carrie wrapped the grey blanket, which somehow didn't feel as rough tonight, around her shoulders.

As the hours slipped by, she focused on her problem. Perhaps she could start again, or maybe Mother would change her mind. Ah! Mother, now that problem required action. At five a.m. she again lay down on the stretcher bed and slept soundly.

The passing days followed the same pattern. The darkness hid her from reality and made her troubles diminish. It felt like a new friend. Surprisingly, the days were filled with sleep.

Aware of the need to make sure it was still all right for her to stay in Bert's shed, Carrie ventured into the café on the fifth day. Pushing hesitantly through the coloured strips, she entered with a shyness not usually attributed to Carolyn Bayley, the heiress of a multi-million-dollar enterprise.

'Hi, Carrie. We wondered when you'd surface.' Patty continued folding paper napkins.

'Sorry, I should have come in sooner. Is it still okay to stay a couple more days?'

'I'm sure it will be.' Patty called to the closed kitchen door. 'Hey, Bert. Carrie wants to stay some more. You don't mind, do you?'

A muffled voice replied in the affirmative.

'Thanks, Bert,' Carrie yelled. She lowered her voice and said to Patty, 'Look, I've also come to apologise. Do you have a moment to talk?'

'Of course, but it's okay. I could tell you were upset.'

Carrie laughed, 'Obvious, was it?'

Patty pointed to the table at the end of the dining area, sat down and waited.

After unnecessarily rearranging the items on the table, Carrie spoke softly. 'I'm having a hard time coming to terms with my mother insisting I'm not good enough to run the family business. My father died and she wants me to sell up.'

Surprised by the revelation, Patty asked, 'What do you want?'

'Me?' Carrie snorted a laugh. 'I've always wanted to run the business. I can, you know. Dad knew it. He trained me. But Mother! Boy, she really has me spitting chips.'

Lost for an opinion on Carrie's worthiness, Patty asked, 'So you're going to stay longer?'

'Yes, I'd like to.' Carrie touched Patty's hand, frowned then said, 'There's something about that place. Sitting on that old wooden jetty surrounded by the universe. Makes you wonder, doesn't it?'

'About what?'

'Everything. I really feel like just a speck in the ocean. Well, lake, if we put it into context.' Carrie's laugh covered her unfamiliar feeling of awkwardness. 'I'm unused to revealing my emotions, you know. Can't have the hired help seeing you out of control.' She shrugged. 'My mother's mantra. Well, one of the many. That's why I had to leave. Get away. Away from anyone I knew.'

'And did you?'

'Of course.'

'Away from even yourself?'

'Me?' Patty's question surprised Carrie. She was unsure how to answer – not many people put Carolyn Bayley on the spot.

'One can't run from oneself. We can't run from our troubles, you know. I'm guessing you haven't got away from yours.'

'Only when I was sitting by the lake.'

Patty nodded, pushed back her chair and announced Bert needed her in the kitchen. 'Bert says it's okay to stay as long as you like. Just call in here before you go.'

Carrie returned to the lake and as the evening became colder she wrapped her shoulders in the blanket and walked to the jetty. The rough pebbles under her feet made her skin tingle with a remembered delight. This was something she hadn't done since she was a small girl. The shallow water covered her feet, chilling them and making her shiver. When she could no longer bear the cold water, she settled herself on the end of the jetty and watched the moon move across the sky.

Morning came. She started back to the boat shed, but with the sun about to fill the sky, it suddenly seemed a shame to spend another day in bed. After a quick shower, she took her coffee and toast and sat in the shade of one of the small trees. The dark colours of the night waters gradually turned an incredible transparent blue. The pebbles shone as the waves slithered to shore. Carrie felt content. She accepted the joy of being in such a wonderful place.

One week later, she faced her mother with a new confidence. The argument over the sale of Bayley Enterprises had been resolved. Carrie decided to accept her share and move on.

It came as a shock to Mrs Bayley that her daughter was going to start a business in some little town hardly more than a speck on the map. What did Carrie Bayley know about fishing? What did her daughter know about boats, tourists and motels?

www.ingramcontent.com/pod-product-compliance
Lightning Source LLC
Chambersburg PA
CBHW020346110726
47898CB00003B/1055